Srotosini Acharjee

CALAMITY:
A TRANSFORMATION

BLUEROSE PUBLISHERS
India | U.K.

Copyright © Srotosini Acharyee 2024

All rights reserved by author. No part of this publication may be reproduced, stored in a retrieval system or transmitted in any form or by any means, electronic, mechanical, photocopying, recording or otherwise, without the prior permission of the author. Although every precaution has been taken to verify the accuracy of the information contained herein, the publisher assume no responsibility for any errors or omissions. No liability is assumed for damages that may result from the use of information contained within.

BlueRose Publishers takes no responsibility for any damages, losses, or liabilities that may arise from the use or misuse of the information, products, or services provided in this publication.

For permissions requests or inquiries regarding this publication,
please contact:

BLUEROSE PUBLISHERS
www.BlueRoseONE.com
info@bluerosepublishers.com
+91 8882 898 898
+4407342408967

ISBN: 978-93-6452-065-2

Cover design: Daksh
Typesetting: Tanya Raj Upadhyay

First Edition: October 2024

To the pillars of my life, Maa and Bubu, this book is for you. Thank you for believing in me.

Rashmit, if you had never convinced me that I could write, I probably would have never been able to word out my feelings. This win is for us.

"And by the way, everything in life is writable about if you have the outgoing guts to do it and the imagination to improvise. The worst enemy to creativity is self-doubt."

- Sylvia Plath, The Unabridged Journals of Sylvia Plath

PREFACE

This poetry book is a brainchild of mine which took more than four years because I was still wondering what could possibly explain my emotions. I am terrible at expressing my emotions but literature has a beautiful way of embracing the silence. Sylvia Plath, John Keats, Anne Sexton, William Wordsworth, Charles Bukowski, Franz Kafka, Dazai Osamu, and I will keep on naming writers who have inspired me to understand one primary emotion –

"Life is a storm and the calamity only hits you when you are ready to accept the transformation."

This book will take you on rollercoaster ride with a teenage girl who is as confused as a squirrel trying to fiddle through good nuts. It is only in certain ways that the girl finds the end but is it worth it?

Not all endings are happy or sad.

Some just have to be accepted.

TABLE OF CONTENTS

CALM BEFORE THE STORM..................1
PRELUDE 2
THE FIRST HIT 4
TO BELONG SOMEWHERE 6
PLETHORA OF PLATONIC (part-1) 8
UNLOVE ME BETTER 10
ECLIPTIC TIDES 11
OLYMPIAN STORM 13
SHOCK WAVE 14
THE FINAL BELL 15

THE STORM 16
INTERLUDE 17
THE HEART-QUAKE 18
WINTER STORM 20
SOUL FORLORN 22
CHAOS OF A HEART 24
PLETHORA OF PLATONIC (part-2) 26
MAZE RUNNER 27
FALSE GOD 29
CHANGING SEASONS 31
TANGENT OF MAKE-BELIEVE 32
TEMPERATURE/MENT 34
DID YOU? 35

MUSE IN A STORM	36
TORPEDO	37

THE AFTERMATH 39

FAREWELL	40
PLACEBO EFFECT	41
ROMAN EMPIRE	43
DECOMPOSITION	44
PLATH'S CHILD	45
PLETHORA OF PLATONIC (part-3)	47
PARADOX	49
DENIAL	50
APOCALYPSE	51

CALM BEFORE THE STORM

PRELUDE

I stayed quiet before,
And I still am.
The raging monster from the deep dark ocean
Is smiling at me.
He called for me
'Let me consume you
You're just going to die when reality hits the shore'.

I smiled back at him and laughed a little
What a joke the monster made
Thinking I would be scared of its ravenous urge.
Dear oh dear, those numb dark eyes,
Wants love and care,
I know you're tired of hiding in the storm.
Embrace me with all your might,
Love, you'll feel the warmth of a mother.
A woman trying to save her lover,
A daughter begging for her father's attention,
A wife smiling through the pain
And a lover killing her feelings.

A storm in front of her eyes,
A storm in her heart.
A calm in the colony,

A chaos in her birth.
A calm before the storm.
A beauty in the pieces.
Of herself, her love,
her ruins and leashes.

THE FIRST HIT

when you told me you didn't love me anymore,
it didn't hurt me.
it didn't feel like i was breaking down.
instead i dissociated.

I dissociated into something.
something i have no idea about.
something that lacks integrity
something of a lost soul in a crowd.

my heart became two.
an eye and a whirlpool.
a destruction over the land.
a friend into a foe's brand.

my soul died.
my eyes lied.
my devastation was threatening
more than those 5 words attending.

i didn't get crushed by the weight of your sighs
i numbed over the silence of the storm
but hey, that's my price.

I am absorbing it, before I burst into flames
Into this fire of despair.
And you were there staring at the sunset
And me, I was drowning in the ocean.

TO BELONG SOMEWHERE

Hiraeth or home,
To belong somewhere, to be known.
My hands are cold,
It's just winter, I told.

Hiraeth or home,
To belong somewhere, to be known.
My eyes look dead,
I just had an uncomfortable night on my bed.

Hiraeth or home,
To belong somewhere, to be known.
Walked miles by myself,
A venture to find oneself.

Hiraeth or home,
To belong somewhere, to be known.
I fell somewhere not apart,
Well, that's what I said to my heart.

Hiraeth or home,
To belong somewhere, to be known.
Shackles have always bound me,
It's self-control, you see.

Hiraeth or home,
To belong somewhere, to be known.
I bleed unfinished sentences,
Words need to cover long distances.

Hiraeth or home,
To belong somewhere, to be known.
A smile on the face to make you believe
That I will live even when I leave.

PLETHORA OF PLATONIC (PART-1)

the morning coffee never brewed this good
as when you compared my existence to it.
neither too hot nor too cold,
I was the perfect sip.

the sun never embraced me as much as you wrapped me in your blanket
your shade was cooler than the rainy nights in which I'd shiver
the perfect room was a myth
until it had you, me - that's us.

holding hands, age lines in trees
you traced my pain back to the root
of the tree that I climbed
when the fruit was not even ripe.

I was in love.
No. I am in love.

You became my spring in the rain, autumn in the winter, summer in the spring and autumn in the summer.

you became seasons in harmony
in a melody of life
near me again and see
strapped to my thighs is a knife.

honesty is a virtue and I won't lie
you are not a lover
just a fitting body
of my morning coffee and secrecy.

you are a curse, I love it so much
I'd rather be poisoned than be Juliet.
that's not impossible
because there was never a more comfortable room
that did not have you and I - that's us.

UNLOVE ME BETTER

rip me apart before you say that you don't love me,
spare me the pain of accepting defeat,
i hope my ears bleed till ringing screams,
kill me with hatred before i hear your voice so sweet.

burn my skin with your curses before you say that you don't love me,
pour the lava over my metal heart,
i hope my skin melts into nothingness,
earth please swallow me before i become an object you discard.

hit my head for a concussion before you say that you don't love me,
let the blood clot over my nerves and veins,
i hope amnesia hits me for the better
before I bawl my eyes out in your lanes.

lastly,
love me so much that before you say that you don't love me,
feed me your cravings and happiness like a potion,
i hope to get mesmerized in this charm so much
so that you leaving seems like the horizon of an ocean.

infinite.
never-ending.
beautiful.

ECLIPTIC TIDES

I love myself.
more in his arms.
better in his words.
best with him.

he taught me to pose a straight smile
the purity in slow paced conversations
my oh my, did he make me love myself
more than my inhibitions.

jesus, he confessed, "I'd want this forever"
and i stressed on "forever" more than ever
every night with a cigarette between fingers
I'd think of our small endeavours.

you kiss me to sleep,
you don't know i cry sometimes
not because I'd never had it
more because I've always lost it.

you hold my hand and lead the way
while kissing my forehead in compassion
i wanted to kiss you and tell you 8 letters
but I think I'll pass on the confrontation.

I know you don't like me,
but I love how you make me feel.
more in your arms.
better in your words.
and best with you.

OLYMPIAN STORM

I love greek mythology
and he has a viper in his hand.
too tempting to be named Hades
I am Persephone, abandoned.

his eyes spark smart
and I'm just a girl
I wish this was more than a fairy tale
and i was his girl.

Aphrodite and Athena fight a melancholic war inside me.
I tell them, his voice rises from the deep trenches of Atlantis.
Aphrodite calls me a masochistic fool.
Athena tells me loving in ignorance is bliss.

Hermes knows I cant tell him this
Nor send a pigeon to quote my heart
So i spill the ink on pages
that were tossed aside to be burnt.

I am just a mortal in love with a god.
well, history repeats as it does.
I wish he knew this wasn't just a piece of literature
it's a heart brimmed in love and touched with curse

SHOCK WAVE

Anxiety and awe wrap me in warmth
As you walk away from me.
More that I see, I learn
You were no better than he.
All the promises made,
And hands clenched hard,
Were rituals of love,
Oh my stupid heart!
How beautifully I danced under the mistletoe,
Till you came, pulled my crown down
And slapped me back to reality.
Now, I have a bruise and a frown.
A bruise on the same cheeks you kissed millions of times
And a frown on the same face you embraced after your crimes.
A broken heart and a syndrome,
To live longer and to love deeper.
To breathe everyday into thoughts clearer.
This chaos is breaking through my calm
And this was meant to cause no harm.
Yet, here I am breathing through the gushing winds
And snoozing my alarm.

THE FINAL BELL

As I call for the storm to hit me,
The final bell rings.
The lighthouse lights up
Warning the people near the sea
 to move further away
But what about me?
Me, who already drowned in the ocean,
Way before the storm hit the shore.
I rode through the violent waves,
Cut through the piercing splashes of water
And entered into the realm of Poseidon.
Truly, I was in search of Medusa who'd turn my heart into stone.
Why, you ask?
A heart of stone be better
Than a beating battered heart.
I drown myself in the sea.
Embracing the cold kiss of Poseidon,
I surrendered myself into this realm of eternal torture
And I let go.
Take me along to the deepest trench
I am sure; it will not cut me deeper than your words.

THE STORM

INTERLUDE

So the energy that died,
Where did it go?
Why is the silence so deafening?
Why does the absence feel like a gaping hole?
Gulping my senses down by every minute
However, here I am.
The noisy wind and the cacophony of the crows somehow disturbed me.
The silence was not silent anymore.
It kept creeping inside me.
Like the dark clouds I could see over from the roof.
I am scared of the thunder.
However, here I am.
I am standing, tripping, probably falling.
Don't try to hold me.
I want to blend in this chaos of a silence
Bleed my veins out on a symphony
Of the leaves rustling
Like every unnerved part of my body shaking.
The calm is not cool.
The storm is not satisfying.
Oh dear, will you carry me away with you
Into the nothingness of happiness?

THE HEART-QUAKE

You didn't notice me
when my swollen eyes
smiled over my puffy cheeks.
well, I don't blame you.
you're not the first to hate my living nightmare of a life.

but you're the first, to love it and leave it.
you're the first, to choose me and hate it.

You didn't feel sorry
when you unapologetically
laughed at my insecurities.
well, I don't blame you.
you're not the first to mock my delusional beliefs.

but you're the first, to save me and leave me to dry.
you're the first, to love me and make me cry.

You were not so happy
when I confessed about my feelings.
well, I don't blame you.
you're not the first to step over my unstable plates of heart.

but you're the first, to live this earthquake and be unhinged.

you're the first, that I wanted to run to because you were one of a kind.

WINTER STORM

snowflakes didn't touch my lips
as your cold hands did,
caressing the beauty of my dry skin,
under the warmth of your breath.
you clenched my hands,
pulled me towards you,
to tell me that it's just the weather that's cold
but i wasn't loved by a snowman, you know who!
the winds slap me with realization
an empty question it roars,
how long will the goodbye last?
you've completed all your chores.
love is not a job,
winter is not just a season.
love is living,
winter is your heart committing treason.
the whisper of the trees are louder in my heart
and my screams are more painful in the dark.
the darkling thrush is scared of the storm
that a rumbling avalanche is born.

im sorry but the bell jar is airtight.
your words don't reach me.
i am not suffocated, i can breathe.

i exist. i love.
it's all in winter.

dear december,
the bell jar is airtight,
break through the whispers and hug me with delight,
that a broken heart can cry,
and a darkling thrush can sing.

SOUL FORLORN

when you told me you loved me,
I couldn't believe it anymore.
why, you ask?
but you don't remember the nights I cried,
the amount of times I sighed.
you don't remember when you lied,
I hugged you and smiled.

you don't remember me faking
my words, my touch, my happiness,
when you asked whether I was okay,
I lied and loved you a little more and me a little less.

it's been ages since I held myself together like this,
for you, for us?
when you held her hand and laughed so hard,
that loving you felt like a poison, a curse.

avalanche of a love, shifted my morals,
you are grey, I'm merely dark,
A shade of shadows with no light,
holding on with all my might.

just tell me once, that my love was worthy
and I'll be gone,

with the smile that I came with,
My soul forlorn?
kiss me like there's no tomorrow
and I'll be gone.
my soul will not be forlorn,
Because there is no other sunrise,
it's only my choked voice, swollen eyes and muffled cries.

CHAOS OF A HEART

The sky roared and so did my heart.
I was never scared of the lightning.
But the wind blew me away.
Brought me closer to my despair
And right near to my most irrational fear.

A white screen in front of me,
Do you think my mind is as fogged as yours?
I have been looking for answers,
Getting past the wistful (feeling)
Getting closer to wishful (thinking).

A chill down my spine.
Weather is so cool.
I wish I had the warmth…
Oh wait! Heliophilia.
I don't love that anymore.

The thunderstorm sweeping over my existence,
Never felt so right.
Until i fell in love with you,
My Zeus.
If only I was your Hera? Rather, your only Hera?

Agnosthesia about you,
Flaring in my mind and head.
I love to dance in the rain,
Probably that is why the drops pierced my skin.
A beautiful desiderium.
Of you, of the thunder and the rain.
Of love, unfathomable yearning and pain.

PLETHORA OF PLATONIC (PART-2)

you still hold my hands
caress my face like it's yours
why does it feel like a sin
when I wait for you for hours?
to press your nose against my cheeks
to almost kiss me
but hold it back for what
and I fall on my knees.
every time that I gazed at you
was it momentarily a lapse in judgement?
still you made me sit on your lap
and I start to drown in your scent.
your humour, your taunts
your fragile fingers,
I am entwined like a vine
for the memory that lingers.
that night when you kissed me for the first time
and your heart didn't race like mine
you asked, "is this right?"
oblivious that you were, it made me cry.
it was a sin to touch you,
yet I was glad to be Persephone
I'd rather count pomegranates
than the days you weren't mine.

MAZE RUNNER

I love someone.
a labyrinth of puzzles and nostalgia.
he is an espresso and I'm decaf.
he might just notice me, i fear.
he snuggles into my chest
my heart skips a beat
he can hear it racing
I can feel his heat.
a gallery of stories
and his mind is a maze
oh, I love being a wanderlust
i wish this weren't a phase.

I have loved someone.
well he's a maneater now.
with his twisted words and crooked dreams
he threw me down.
he was a magnet
and I'm iron.
i couldn't stand being away
and he couldn't tolerate me alone.
he threw the string
i barely caught it,
and then I tripped

cuz he had already left.
yet he came back
kissed me to life,
sleeping princess was stabbed again
by the beloved's knife.

I loved someone.
he is expired milk
and I'm a beggar.
I am grateful for the bare minimum
that he had to offer.
he still took his hands
placed into mine
under the blanket
where I was always crying.
he never wiped my tears
didn't want me any near
i am picasso's schizophrenic art
and he is a wildflower.

FALSE GOD

how did it feel to run to her
when I was already used for?
you pushed me away so far
and then, ran across my heart's door?
into her's?
into her house?
into her sacred body and scared heart?
of losing a friend with innumerable doubts.
touch her and I burn,
kiss her and I melt,
embrace her and I break,
hold her and I am dead.
not dead, literally
but in front of you.
those tears won't fall anymore,
my smile will fade.
"I love you" - I hate it.
"I miss you" - I crave it.
how much did it take for you to act
like I was nothing
and your feelings weren't there?
when I remember the nights you came running back to me

just so you could kiss me back to sleep and play with my hair?

it was just for a month, but felt like a lifetime.
of love, of happiness, of pure belongingness.
it was just for a moment but felt like you were mine.
of vulnerability, of beauty, of safe space.

touch me and I live,
kiss me and I thrive,
embrace me and I breathe,
hold me and I die.
die in love.
die in faith.
I'll choose you to love forever,
and be an endless "careless whisper".
"I love you" - I miss it.
"I miss you" - I love it.

CHANGING SEASONS

love has not been kind.
love has been transient.
it never stayed to reciprocate alike
it always made me lament.
the truth is, I'm a human
a connoisseur in heartache
and you are a soul
brimmed with namesake.
the invisible string I pulled back
you cut it midway
because you loved the fabric
and i loved the array.
i decorated my arms
with art alike
which you were scared of
but loved to hold a knife.
i am a desperate product
of your dreams desolate
and you are the expectation
my delusion created.
i am the beast
and you are the hunter
I have failed in love again
i am in the gutter.

TANGENT OF MAKE-BELIEVE

the way you held my face
made me shy away from your gaze
yet you say "I'm joking"
while leaving my heart minutely broken.

you come back to me,
tugging at the invisible string
and i despise my heart
that lets you in.

you call me when I breakdown
I hate that I pick up.
you proudly calm me down,
and whisper that I am enough.

however
she is your red string (apparently)
she is your fate (probably)
I am invisible (absolutely)
and vulnerable like my string (desperately)
decimated by my hate.

10 things I hate about you
9 times I'd lie
8 pm we turned apart

7 more days and I died.
6 sunrises by myself
5 pegs of rum
4 minutes of self-loathing
3 nights I was harmed.
2 seconds of crying
1 day of acceptance
0 that made me realise,
I lost my senses.

TEMPERATURE/MENT

I am coffee
Room temperature
Just how you like it
a chaotic piece of literature?

Neither too hot
Neither too cold
Just how you like it
but a bit too bold?

Perfect in taste
Not so bitter
Just how you like it
this is what you whispered.

I don't wait for you to sip on it anymore.
You left me to cool for too long.
I don't cry over my mess anymore.
I know that at least I wasn't in the wrong.

So, your coffee is wasted
And so is the price.
The once warm heart
Has turned into ice.
The love that was fire,
Has died over time.
And you, my love,
not anymore a part of my rhyme.

DID YOU?

when the nights don't seem warm anymore,
when beauty crashes over the horizon,
kisses the stars
and the moon lights up her eyes,
did you see the sparkling sadness,
trickling down her radiant face.

when her hands turn cold,
shivering in sheer anxiety,
her head rings in sore pain,
when the sun burns her skin
more than the cigarettes she butted on her belly,
did you see her wearing pullovers
trying to keep the facade of being so normal?

when she only smiles on your text,
blushes over your compliments,
a twin flame emerges in her,
when her only source of fun becomes a pretended version of you,
did you see her being honest with herself,
loving herself through her eternal storms?

MUSE IN A STORM

to reminisce about all the moments lost,
I still have your touch engraved in my soul.
a part of me that'll never be mine anymore
a slit over a bullet hole.

the breaths still tingle my skin
as if it was a storm on a desolated land
clear as a day do I remember
the second you let go of my hand

for a moment everything was hazy,
a cloud over my moral scriptures
yet I couldn't know how to get past them
so I cried about it for hours

deadly as it is,
like a tanto in my hand
I carved this feeling out of blood
and of emotions in a dead heart.

TORPEDO

When you said my home was with you,
Did you mean the house we live in or me?
Because both of us are dilapidated,
I didn't know where you wanted to return.

My embrace wasn't warm enough,
Neither was the kitchen fire lit all the time,
where did you find the solace?
Wait, was I just a passion crime?

You used to kiss me and tell me repeatedly,
That you want to come home with me
But where did you live inside me?
Head or heart?
Or rather where did I live?
Your home or my body?

When you said my home was with you,
Did you mean to abandon it?
Or did you just find a new home?
Where it isn't with me?
Where I am just a memory in the walls.
I am just in your essence,
Just your words,
And just a beautiful story.

Tell me I am your home again,
And I might cry
Because broken homes are only houses.
It's made of love iced in a lie.

THE AFTERMATH

FAREWELL

goodbyes aren't always beautiful.
sometimes, they leave scars.
just like the one you said,
vanishing away like a shooting star!

I remained standing at the door.
Waiting for that one last glimpse
With tears down my cheeks;
and disappearing links.

for once, the art of letting go,
that I mastered over the years,
started pinching my soul
And i got overwhelmed by my fears.

this distasteful heart of mine,
never felt so wrong,
in letting a person go,
as it did for you.
I wonder what it is?
love, affection, craving, desire
or merely the fact that,
You taught me how to live,
while I was just existing.

PLACEBO EFFECT

Do I still miss you after everything?
certainly a no.
probably a yes.

those long stares into my eyes while I slept,
when asked you'd say, "I wanna drown in your depth".
I used to hide away.
But you'd hold my hand and say, "Your eyes speak what you can't, and I can see it, bright as day!"

my hungry heart couldn't wait to gobble until I got home
to you, and there you were,
with two plates full of food and happy eyes.
And I was there.
I loved that you were so nice.

midnight movies, extreme breakdowns,
days of fighting and acting like clowns,
millennial songs and boomer conversations,
you wrapped in a blanket of warm imagination.

friends to lovers to jealousy,
my favourite trope, you see?

I miss you, that ain't a lie,
I don't miss us, and that's why I cry.

Do I still miss you after everything?
certainly a no.
probably a yes.

ROMAN EMPIRE

i wasn't exactly a perfect model
of how you'd love me like Vincent loved his paint
I'm rather a ruin of sorts like Roman art caressed too much
I've begged you to love me so much
I think I believe my mother's hunch.

astronomy, literature, The Orion and Achilles,
how you'd compare my flaws to the moon's crevices
now I'm a bothering old neighbour with too much to tell
and you're counting my days.

You kissed me so hard I could feel my soul sucked in.
Never felt that unless I thought you'd be the Grim Reaper
Maybe I'm not that wrong, with the demon you are
your disguise as an angel was cleaner.

DECOMPOSITION

most of the time I just feel empty;
not the box-empty
but the field-empty
vast lands of twisted love and happiness
not to belong to anyone
but mine to suffer and bear
until I give up.

there is something fundamentally absent in me.
it's a hollow space into a wonderland
except an Alice because I am the Mad Hatter.
I stay pensive, trying to ponder over my happy memories
however, all I reach is an illusion of the end.

how many times did I blow air and not pour water over the fire inside me?
when everything is ashes and pain doesn't define its beauty?
now, I'm just a relic of all the empty smiles that I showed to people.
I'm just a memoir of dead memories that have not decayed.

PLATH'S CHILD

oh how I'd love to be my dad's favourite
dear lord where did my birth go wrong?
from the blood and sweat of my mother
and my dad, headstrong?
I wanted him to see me as his daughter
not as a wager for his respect
what price did the father in heaven put on me
that I was sold off for intellect?

oh how I'd love to be my dad's favourite
close enough to a son if can be
so that his words don't sting my heart
and his gazes couldn't really see
how broken of a daughter have i become
in this sensitivity of being a forgery.

oh how I'd love to be my dad's favourite
only if I was his own
my mother makes it believable
that he had a heart to loan.
i smiled over a drop rolling down
because my heart was breaking
over his love to my mom
but his mocking towards my wins.

oh how I'd love to be my dad's favourite
only if I followed the path he asked me to
like the rational choices of life
and build my tissues anew.
But I was my mother's daughter,
bleeding for validation everyday
I was a cut-throat vixen
with ideas on play.

except I was never his favourite
i was just a possession.
I was never his daughter to be
but a son that I can never be.

PLETHORA OF PLATONIC (PART-3)

"we are just friends" but
your hand on my hand - is platonic, you said.
"we are just friends" but
you like my kiss on your forehead.
"we are just friends" but
you want to share your food with me.
"we are just friends" but
you like me better because I just let you be.
"we are just friends" but
my hair is your favourite smell.
"we are just friends" but
you'd sin for me to ride to hell.
"we are just friends" but
you wipe my tears and let me scream.
"we are just friends" but
spotify has our blended stream.
"we are just friends" but
you hate any guy I like.
"we are just friends" but
you love when we end our fights.
"we are just friends" but
you've disappeared on me time and time again
"we are just friends" but

I've waited for you to come back the same.
"we are just friends" but
you love our invisible string.
"we are just friends" but
Every time I left the city, you gave me your precious ring.
"we are just friends" but
you've caressed me secretly.
"we are just friends" but
I have loved you bitterly.
"we are just friends" but
you know every part of me.
"we are just friends" but
a kiss was all I needed to feel.
"we are just friends" and
i don't want that anymore.
"we are just friends" and
I will love you till my heart is sore.

PARADOX

you need me and I can't let you go
it's a funny paradox actually

because neither i remember you holding me back
nor me begging persistently.

because neither i remember you choosing me first
nor you being my priority.

because neither i remember you crying on rough days
nor me asking you hesitantly.

because neither i remember you calling me first after
your blind date
nor me drinking responsibly.

because neither i remember you promising to stay in
touch
nor me watching each minute consistently.

because neither i remember you being the same
person whom I fell in love with
nor me who loved you ardently.

you need me and I can't let you go
it's a funny paradox actually.

DENIAL

i wake up blind
to my inhibitions and ambitions
I am a mechanical corpse
to my present inspiration.

my values collide
i dive into your lies
my morals don't exist
my belief still persists.

my tears don't roll down
i wipe it off
I don't cry no more
I am mostly lost.

I rest my head down.
I take a deep breath.
I smile a little
and wear a red dress..

APOCALYPSE

It's like the sand that slipped through,
A momentary lapse into a trance,
It's like the sky that kissed the sunset
An apocalypse that crash-landed at a distance.

The smoke is burning me,
It left patches of bruised love.
Dear, don't hold my hand
I have had scars to write of.
A part of my story,
A part of my soul,
A fragment of belief,
I don't want to hold.
A melody that will never fade away,
You'll be stuck like that one bridge of a song
That breaks into infinite pieces
But brings peace with the end of the storm.

Like the destructive hurricane,
Like the dilapidated house,
Like the goodbye never returned,
Like the eyes that wept dry,
Like the first dew touching your cheeks,
Like the sun that always burns you,

Like the rain that doesn't make you smile anymore,
Like the autumn that leaves you dead,
Like the winter which will kill and the spring which will mock,
You left traces of your desperate cravings everywhere.

The times you couldn't stand up anymore,
I know you pushed yourself too.
You will tear down walls every wall between us.
I will take everything that is due.

The apocalypse changes everything.
I am just a house with roots so tender,
As I break, I don't know
Whether you are being rude or kinder?

You're that apocalypse.
I am running from it.
I look back and I still don't know
Did you save or sacrifice yourself in this?

Like Osho Jain said, 'Tu aisa kaise hain?' (*how are you like this?*)

www.ingramcontent.com/pod-product-compliance
Lightning Source LLC
LaVergne TN
LVHW041225080526
838199LV00083B/3365